Jack and the Beanstalk

illustrated by Robert McPhillips

Jack and his mother were very poor. All they had was one cow.

One day, Jack's mother said, "Go and sell our cow and bring the money back to me."

This book belongs to:

_____

A catalogue record for this book is available from the British Library

Published by Ladybird Books Ltd
A Penguin Company
Penguin Books Ltd, 80 Strand, London WC2R 0RL, UK
Penguin Books Australia Ltd, Camberwell, Victoria, Australia
Penguin Group (NZ) Ltd, 67 Apollo Drive, Rosedale, North Shore 0632, New Zealand

8 10 9 7
© LADYBIRD BOOKS LTD MCMXCVIII. This edition MMVI
ILLUSTRATIONS © ROBERT MCPHILLIPS MCMXCVIII

ISBN-13: 978-1-84422-930-7

Printed in China

5

Jack took the cow away to sell. On the way he met a man who wanted to buy the cow.

"I have no money," said the man. "But I will give you five magic beans for your cow."

"All right," said Jack, and he gave the man his cow.

Jack took the beans back to his mother. She was very angry.

"These beans are no good to us," she said. And she threw the beans out of the window.

The next day when Jack woke up, he saw a giant beanstalk outside his window.

"I want to climb to the top," said Jack.

Jack started to climb the beanstalk.

"No, Jack, no!" said Jack's mother, but Jack climbed up and up and up to the very top of the beanstalk.

Jack saw a giant castle with a giant door. When he opened the door he saw a giant woman.

"Look out!" said the woman. "My husband is coming. He will eat you up!"

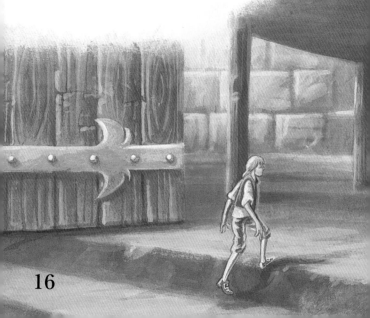

"Fee fi fo fum, watch out everyone, HERE I COME," roared the giant.

"You must hide," said the woman. And she hid Jack in a cupboard.

The giant came in and sat down at the table with some giant bags of money. He started to count his money. Jack watched him from inside the cupboard.

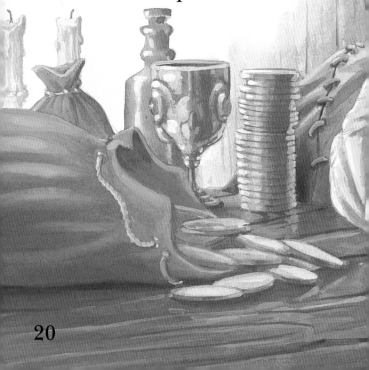

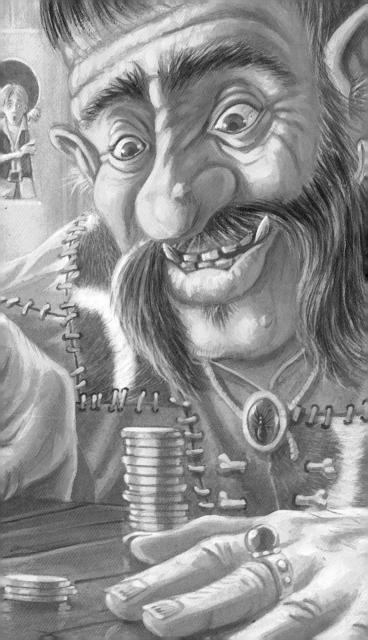

Soon, the giant fell asleep. Jack came out of the cupboard and took all the money. Then he climbed down the beanstalk, and gave the money to his mother.

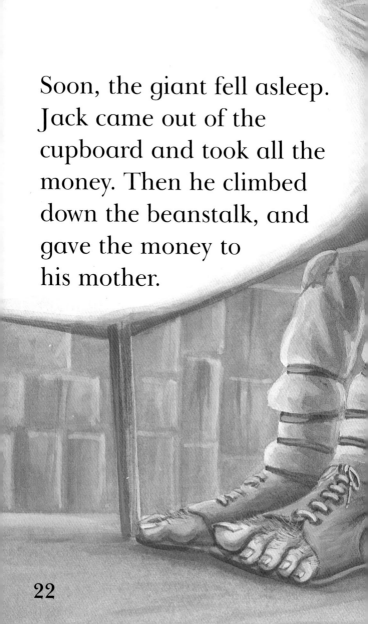

Not long after, Jack wanted to climb the beanstalk again.

"No, Jack, no!" said his mother. But Jack said, "I must."

Jack saw the giant woman again.

"Look out!" she said. "My husband is angry because his money has been stolen."

"Fee fi fo fum, watch out everyone, HERE I COME!" roared the giant.

27

"You must hide in the cupboard," said the woman.

The giant came in and sat down at the table. He had with him a magic hen. The magic hen laid golden eggs.

Very soon, the giant fell asleep. Jack came out of the cupboard and took the hen. Then he climbed down the beanstalk.

The next day, Jack climbed the beanstalk again. At the top of the beanstalk, Jack saw the giant woman.

33

"Look out!" said the woman.
"My husband is angry
because his hen and his
money have been stolen."

"Fee fi fo fum, watch out
everyone, HERE I COME!"
roared the giant.

"You must hide in the cupboard again," said the woman.

The giant came in with a magic harp. He sat down at the table and the harp started to play.

Soon, the giant fell asleep.
Jack came out of the
cupboard and took the harp.
Then he started to climb
down the beanstalk.

"Run away!" said the woman.
"The giant is behind you!"

Jack climbed down the beanstalk with the angry giant behind him. When Jack was at the bottom, his mother cut down the beanstalk.

CRASH! And that was the end of the giant.

Now Jack and his mother were not poor, and they lived happily ever after.

Read It Yourself is a series of graded readers designed to give young children a confident and successful start to reading.

Level 3 is suitable for children who are developing reading confidence and stamina, and who are ready to progress to longer stories with a wider vocabulary. The stories are told simply and with a richness of language.

About this book

At this stage of reading development, it's rewarding to ask children how they prefer to approach each new story. Some children like to look first at the pictures and discuss them with an adult. Some children prefer the adult to read the story to them before they attempt it for themselves. Many children at this stage will be eager to read the story aloud to an adult at once, and to discuss it afterwards. Unknown words can be worked out by looking at the beginning letter (*what sound does this letter make?*) and the sounds the child recognises within the word. The child can then decide which word would make sense.

Developing readers need lots of praise and encouragement.